W9-DCU-182

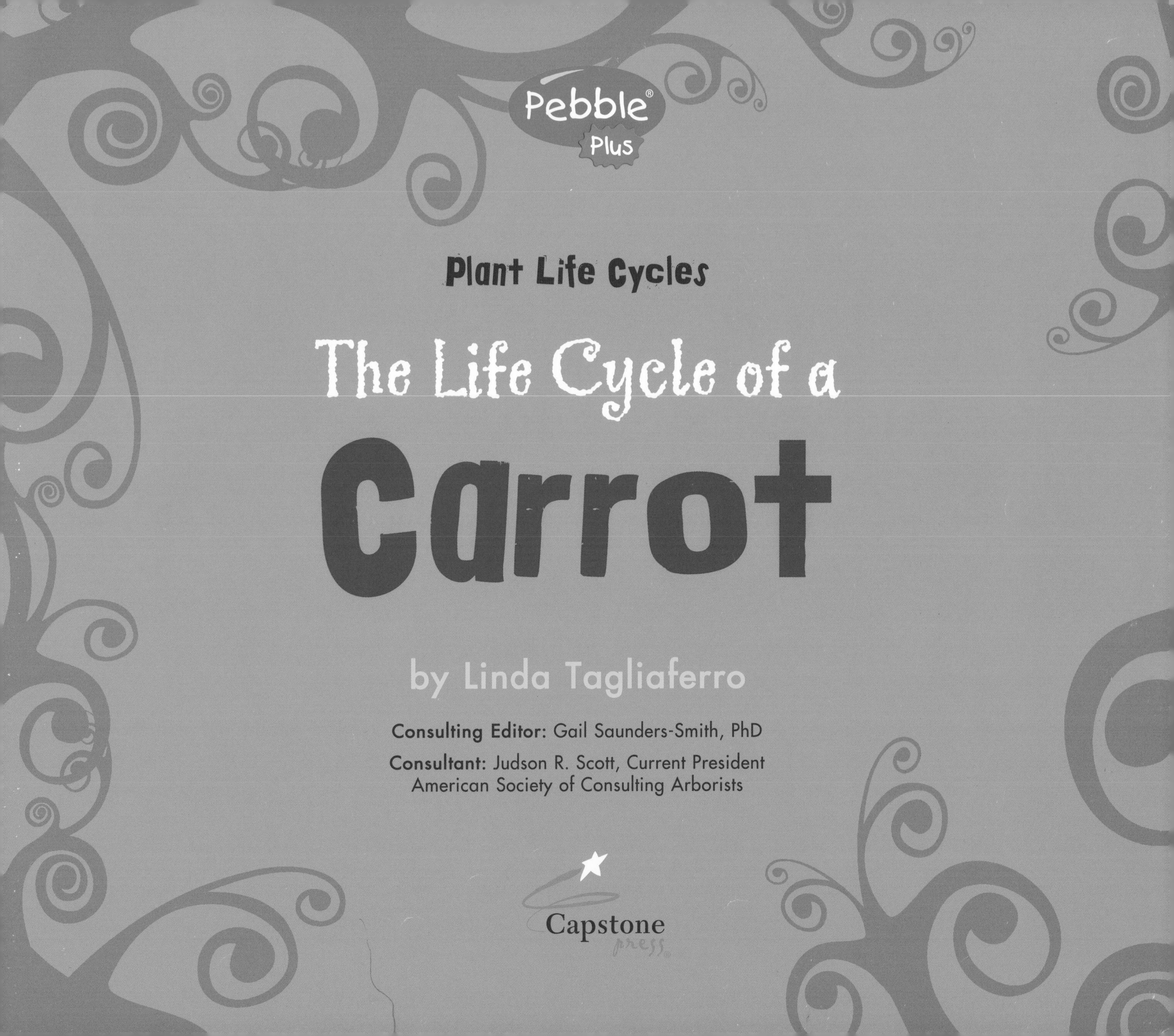

Pebble® Plus

Plant Life Cycles

# The Life Cycle of a Carrot

by Linda Tagliaferro

**Consulting Editor:** Gail Saunders-Smith, PhD

**Consultant:** Judson R. Scott, Current President
American Society of Consulting Arborists

Capstone press

Pebble Plus is published by Capstone Press,
151 Good Counsel Drive, P.O. Box 669, Mankato, Minnesota 56002.
www.capstonepress.com


Printed in the United States of America

1 2 3 4 5 6 12 11 10 09 08 07

*Library of Congress Cataloging-in-Publication Data*
Tagliaferro, Linda.
The life cycle of a carrot / by Linda Tagliaferro.
p. cm.—(Pebble plus. Plant life cycles)
Summary: "Simple text and photographs present the life cycle of a carrot plant from seed to adult"—Provided by publisher.
Includes bibliographical references and index.
ISBN-13: 978-07368-6713-9 (hardcover)
ISBN-10: 0-7368-6713-9 (hardcover)
1. Carrots—Life cycles—Juvenile literature. I. Title. II. Series.
SB351.C3 T34 2007
635.13—dc22 2006020941

**Editorial Credits**
Sarah L. Schuette, editor; Bobbi J. Wyss, set designer; Jo Miller, photo researcher/photo editor

**Photo Credits**
Art Directors/Helene Rogers, cover (small plant), 5, 21 (small plant)
David Liebman © David Liebman Pink Guppy, 7, 9, 15, 17, 19
Grant Heilman Photography, 11; B. Runk/S. Schoenberger, 20 (germinating seed); Cynthia Lujan, 21 (carrots)
Shutterstock/Graca Victoria, cover (soil); photocay, cover (carrots)
SuperStock/Michael P. Gadomski, 13
Visuals Unlimited/Scientifica, cover (seeds), 20 (seeds)

## Note to Parents and Teachers

The Plant Life Cycles set supports national science standards related to the life cycles of plants and animals. This book describes and illustrates the life cycle of a carrot. The images support early readers in understanding the text. The repetition of words and phrases helps early readers learn new words. This book also introduces early readers to subject-specific vocabulary words, which are defined in the Glossary section. Early readers may need assistance to read some words and to use the Table of Contents, Glossary, Read More, Internet Sites, and Index sections of the book.

# Table of Contents

# Carrot Seeds

How do carrots grow?
Carrots grow from seeds
that are planted in the soil.

Carrot seeds need water and warmth to sprout.

# Growing

Carrot seeds grow roots
under the ground.
Thin stems and green leaves
grow above the ground.

Carrot roots get thicker
and thicker underground.
The root is the part we eat.

# Carrots!

After 60 days,
the carrots are pulled up
by their tops.

Some carrot plants stay
in the ground all winter.
Flowers bloom on the plants
the next spring.

Bees carry pollen
from flower to flower.
Pollen helps new seeds
grow inside flowers.

## Starting Over

In fall, carrot flowers bend
and the seeds fall out.
The seeds can grow
into new carrots.
The life cycle continues.

# How Carrots Grow

young plants
carrots

# Glossary

**life cycle**—the stages in the life of a plant that include sprouting, reproducing, and dying

**pollen**—the tiny, yellow grains made by flowers; pollen helps new flowers grow.

**root**—the part of a plant that grows mostly underground; the roots of the carrot plant are called carrots.

**seed**—the part of a flowering plant that can grow into a new plant

**sprout**—to grow, appear, or develop quickly; sprouting seeds make roots and stems.

# Read More


**Bodach, Vijaya**. *Roots.* Plant Parts. Mankato, Minn.: Capstone Press, 2007.

**James, Ray**. *Plant Cycle.* Nature's Cycle. Vero Beach, Fla.: Rourke, 2007.

**Snyder, Inez**. *Carrots.* Harvesttime. New York: Children's Press, 2004.


# Internet Sites

FactHound offers a safe, fun way to find Internet sites related to this book. All of the sites on FactHound have been researched by our staff.

Here's how:

1. Visit *www.facthound.com*
2. Choose your grade level.
3. Type in this book ID **0736867139** for age-appropriate sites. You may also browse subjects by clicking on letters, or by clicking on pictures and words.
4. Click on the **Fetch It** button.

**FactHound will fetch the best sites for you!**

# Index



Word Count: 115
Grade: 1
Early-Intervention Level: 14